The Ballad of Knuckles McGraw

ORCA
YOUNG
READERS

The Ballad of
Knuckles McGraw

LOIS PETERSON

ORCA BOOK PUBLISHERS

Library and Archives Canada Cataloguing in Publication

Peterson, Lois J., 1952-

The ballad of Knuckles McGraw / written by Lois Peterson.

ISBN 978-1-55469-203-3

I. Title.

PS8631.E832B34 2010   jC813'.6   C2009-906876-1

First published in the United States, 2010
Library of Congress Control Number: 2009940935

Summary: After Kevin's mother abandons him, he takes refuge in his fantasy of becoming a cowboy, but his reality is a foster home and grandparents he doesn't know.

Orca Book Publishers gratefully acknowledges the support for its publishing programs provided by the following agencies: the Government of Canada through the Canada Book Fund and the Canada Council for the Arts, and the Province of British Columbia through the BC Arts Council and the Book Publishing Tax Credit.

Typesetting by Bruce Collins
Cover artwork by Peter Ferguson
Author photo by E. Henry

ORCA BOOK PUBLISHERS
PO Box 5626, STN. B
VICTORIA, BC CANADA
V8R 6S4

ORCA BOOK PUBLISHERS
PO Box 468
CUSTER, WA USA
98240-0468

www.orcabook.com
Printed and bound in Canada.
Printed on 100% PCW recycled paper.

13 12 11 10 • 4 3 2 1

For Holly and Brad—and Adam, of course!

Contents

CHAPTER 1

Boxcars and Cabooses

Kevin Mason sits in the car watching the train rumble by. Next to him, the welfare lady taps her fingers on the steering wheel. He can't remember her name. Or maybe she forgot to tell it to him when she came to fetch him from school.

His hands are warm and damp around the handle of his Wagon Train lunch box. When he chose it at the thrift store, his mom told him that it might be an antique. It might be worth something. His mother is always taking stuff to the pawnshop to get money for tomato soup and cigarettes. So ever since he caught her checking it out with a greedy look on her face, Kevin has made sure he and his Wagon Train lunch box stick together.

"Put that on the floor if you like," the welfare lady tells him. She is in a big hurry. At the school, she had talked quickly in a very quiet voice to the principal. Her shoes made tapping sounds on the sidewalk as she led Kevin to her car. She talked so fast while he buckled up that he only just made out that she was telling him that she was taking him to a foster family for the night.

He tries not to think of that now. It hurts somewhere down in his stomach to be stuck with this strange lady, going someplace he has never been before, when he should be home waiting for his mom to get back from work.

His eyes follow the boxcars. He lost track at twenty-seven, but there's still a whole bunch to come.

His ears fill with squeals and clanks and grinding noises as the train rumbles over the shiny tracks. The lady's fingers are still busy, moving along the grooves of the steering wheel, tapping in time to the sound of the bell that rings and rings and rings to warn them to wait at the railroad crossing until the train is gone.

Kevin holds his lunch box tight against his chest. He let his school principal and this lady read his mother's note. But he asked for it back right away. It is now wrapped around the peanut butter and jelly sandwich, the way he found it.

The boxcars lumber past. When the last one goes by, he will wave to the trainman sitting by the open window with his elbow sticking out. He always waves whenever he waits for trains to go by. But trainmen hardly ever wave back.

"It's not far," the lady tells him. "It won't take long to get there."

Kevin keeps looking out the car window so he does not have to look at her or her tidy black suit and shiny dark hair. Instead, his eyes keep following the bumping boxcars. Graffiti is scrawled on the side of one. He sees the big *K* and the big *M* first.

His initials! He turns in his seat so he can read the whole thing before the boxcar judders away. It says *Knuckles McGraw*.

Kevin rolls the words around and around in his head. *Knuckles McGraw* sounds like the name of a cowboy who rides the range. A cowboy with beef jerky in his back pocket and a can of beans stuffed in his saddlebag. A cowboy who wears a hat with a greasy string hanging down the front of his shirt, and boots with rattling spurs. One who carries a red bandanna to spit into whenever he feels like it.

He can spell *bandanna* backward and forward. A-N-N-A-D-N-A-B. He has been the best speller in every class, in every school he has been in. Later he will figure out how to spell *Knuckles McGraw* backward too.

More rusty red boxcars grind by. *Burlington Northern* is written on most of them. *Burlington Northern. Burlington Northern. Burlington Northern. Burlington Northern.*

That would be a really good name for a horse, Kevin thinks. If he was a cowboy called Knuckles McGraw, he would call his horse Burlington for short. He would leap onto his back without needing a hand up. He'd grab the reins and lean low over the saddle as he rode into the night, leaving behind the busy principal and the welfare lady, who is nice in a way that makes Kevin Mason want to cry.

But cowboys don't cry. A cowboy with supper in his saddlebag and a horse called Burlington Northern has nothing to cry about.

Right there and then, he decides that from now on he will be Knuckles McGraw, riding the range. Instead of Kevin Mason, whose mom left a note in his Wagon Train lunch box that said *Please look after my son. I can't take care of him anymore.*

CHAPTER 2

Meet the Family

When they get where they are going, Knuckles McGraw stays in the passenger seat holding his lunch box on his lap while the welfare lady gets out of the car. However hard he tries to keep his eyes looking ahead at the cars lined up along the sidewalk, they drift sideways when she opens his door. "Come and meet the family," she says.

A string of fish-shaped lights is hung along the porch at the top of the wide steps. The front door opens, and a tall thin man comes out.

"I know him," Knuckles McGraw says.

"I don't think so," the welfare lady says. He can tell she isn't really listening to him.

"He comes to my school sometimes," Knuckles McGraw insists. The man has a ponytail. "He always wears plaid shirts."

"Perhaps. Now come along." When Knuckles McGraw slides out, she puts one hand in the middle of his back to lead him up the stairs.

"Hello. I'm Joe," says the man.

"I am just here for a few days." Knuckles McGraw wants to say more, but the words are all tied around his tongue. And he doesn't know how to untangle them.

"Let's go inside." Joe steps aside. Kevin Mason's mom has taught him Ladies First. So Knuckles McGraw stands next to the man to let the welfare lady walk past sideways. Then he and Joe follow her into the house.

In the kitchen, a girl sits with one bare foot propped on the table, where little bottles stand in a row. As she dips a brush carefully in one, her tongue peeks out from between her teeth.

"We have company, Breeze," Joe says.

Knuckles McGraw stands next to the table, waiting to say hello. But the girl with the funny name just strokes pearly blue polish onto one nail. She puts the brush back into the bottle and screws the lid on.

When Joe says "Bree-zy," in a warning kind of way, she waggles her fingers in a little wave. She looks at the welfare lady. Then she gets up and stands in front of Knuckles McGraw. She stares at him without blinking. She is very pale and very thin.

"You go to my school," he says. He has seen her in the other grade-three class. When he looks at the floor, he sees that each nail on one of Breezy's feet is a different color. She hasn't painted her other toes yet.

"Where's Liddy?" Joe asks. The girl points at the back door. "You'll meet her in a bit, Kevin," says Joe. "She'll be out in her workshop. Liddy and I are Breezy's grandparents. Breezy, show Kevin where he will sleep tonight while Ms. Havers and I have a bit of a chat."

Knuckles McGraw doesn't move until the lady gives him a little nod and says, "Go ahead."

"My name is Knuckles McGraw," he tells the girl as he follows her out of the room. But she doesn't answer.

As he follows Breezy's bare feet up the stairs, he looks at the pictures that run up the wall above the railing. They are all in thick, fancy frames. A kid's drawing is in each one. All the drawings are of the same two people. A woman with long hair and big blue eyes. A man with dark hair and a mustache. But the pictures are all different. In one the lady is wearing a blue shirt, and in another a red dress. The man is wearing round glasses in one. In the one next to it, his glasses are square.

"Who are those people?" he asks Breezy, who is waiting for him at the top.

She blinks at him, but doesn't answer. She just turns away and leads him down the hall, where she opens a door and lets him go in ahead of her.

A cowboy would share a bunkhouse with other cowboys, thinks Knuckles McGraw. This room has just two beds. Breezy plunks herself down on one and starts bouncing on it. The springs creak. A pillow falls off.

The bed on the other side of the room is all rumpled. The mat beside it is half tucked under. And all over the walls above the bed hang pictures torn out of magazines.

Knuckles McGraw moves closer to study them. Each one is of an iceberg. Huge and cold blue.

Some with cracks, some with the sea lapping against the sides. In one picture a huge chunk of ice is falling into the sea, making a giant wave. "Whose bed is this?" he asks Breezy.

She is standing on her head on the other bed. Her painted toes look like petals on her white stalk legs. She doesn't answer.

"Is it yours?" he asks.

She flips over and lands with a thump on the mattress. She rolls off and sighs, staring at him with her hands on her hips. She pads across the room and points to a poster on the wall at the head of the bed. One word is written in sharp pointy writing like lightning. *ICE*.

"I know it's ice," he says.

She shakes her head and makes a face as if it's the dumbest thing she's ever heard. She pokes her finger at the sign. Then she pats the pillow.

Suddenly, loud footsteps thunder up the stairs. Breezy moves back against the bed just as the door swings open. Knuckles McGraw is left standing in the middle of the room.

CHAPTER 3

Waifs and Strays

"What do we have here?" A teenage boy thumps into the room and throws himself on the bed. He's wearing a black leather jacket with chains down the sleeves. His hair is the color that Knuckles McGraw's mother once dyed hers when he was still Kevin Mason— a black that is almost blue. It sticks up in shiny points. "Another waif and stray?" the boy asks. He looks from Knuckles McGraw to Breezy. A ring is stuck through his bottom lip, and the flickery silver of a tongue stud shows when he speaks.

The girl nods and moves back to the other bed, where she stands on one foot with her hip resting against the mattress.

"I am not a wife," Knuckles McGraw tells the boy in leather. "And I'm not a stray. I was brought here until my mom comes back to get me."

The boy raises his eyebrows. "They all say that. 'It won't be long,' they say. 'It's just for a while.' 'I'll be going home soon,' they say. Well, however long it takes, you stick to your side, hear?"

He roots in the drawer of his bedside table and pulls out a piece of chalk. It's thick, like the stuff girls use for sidewalk hopscotch. Ice pushes past Knuckles McGraw and bends over in the middle of the room, where he draws a long straight line. Right down the center of the carpet. He points to the side with the empty bed. "That marks your territory. Got it?"

"Okay. I mean, got it."

"Glad we have that straight. I am Ice," the boy tells him. "My real name"—his eyes go all slanty—"which no one in this house is allowed to use under threat of dire punishment, is not for you to know. Just call me Ice. I-C-E. Get it?"

Knuckles looks at the wall covered with pictures of icebergs. Then back at the boy and his leather and studs. He nods.

"Well?" the boy asks.

Breezy slips out of the room.

"Well?" says Ice again. "Please tell me I'm not stuck with another dumb kid. You could reciprocate. Tell me…"

"I know what reciprocate means," Knuckles McGraw tells him. "I can spell it forward and backward. I can spell almost every word in the dictionary forward and backward. E-T-A-C-O-R-P-I-C-E-R."

"What am I, on *Jeopardy*?" When Ice sits on the side of his bed, the chains on his jacket jangle.

"My name is Knuckles McGraw."

Ice nods slowly. "Way cool, man." He reaches into the inside pocket of his jacket and pulls out a piece of paper. He unfolds it carefully, then smoothes it out on his bedcovers. "*National Geographic,*" he says. "The library's reference copy. No one will ever miss it." He reaches into his drawer again and brings out a tack with a red head. He pins his picture on the wall.

This iceberg does not look much different than the others.

"Your name is weird," says Knuckles McGraw.

"Look who's talking," says the boy. "By the way, Joe says to come downstairs. Chow time." Ice slaps his hand against the new picture on his wall and heads out of the room.

"Way cool," says Knuckles McGraw under his breath. Cowboys in a bunkhouse would say "Chow time." He tucks his lunch box tightly under his arm and follows Ice out of the room. Rude words are written in silver marker all down the back of the boy's black jeans.

Knuckles McGraw reads them aloud in his head, without moving his lips, in case anyone sees.

CHAPTER 4

Five for Supper

In the kitchen, the welfare lady has gone. Breezy is back in her chair rearranging her bottles of nail polish. The man called Joe stands at the stove stirring something in a big pot.

At the table sits a woman whose hair is as short as a man's. It's sprinkled with sawdust, like brown dandruff. "Nice to have you here." She smiles. "I see you got acquainted with Breezy and Ice. You are Knuckles, I hear." She nods. "Interesting name."

"The names go together," he tells her. "It's Knuckles McGraw."

"Hmm. I see." She turns to the man. "Joe? Do we have a rule that children with regular names like

Sharon and Brian and Philip are not welcome here? Or is that just the way it turns out?"

When the man laughs, his ponytail shifts on his back.

"I am Liddy, Breezy's grandmother," she tells Knuckles McGraw. "You're going to stay with us for a bit until we track down your mom. Get things sorted out."

He swallows the lump in his throat. Cowboys don't cry, not even when they think about their mothers. "Okay."

"Can you put your lunch box on the counter?"

He puts both arms around it and holds it to his chest.

"You can clean it out after supper," says Liddy as she stands up and shuffles the chairs around the table. "Breezy, get that stinking stuff out of here. Ice—cutlery." She looks at Ice with her hands on her hips. "I thought you had chores today. Where have you been?"

"At the library." When Ice winks at him, Knuckles McGraw notices that next to the boy's eye is a tattoo of a tiny blue tear.

"Fancy that," says Liddy. "But you know the drill. Chores first. Friends and the skateboard park and movies later. And the library too. Try to remember."

Ice growls something that Knuckles McGraw can't make out and hands him a bunch of knives and forks as if they were flowers. *"Contribute to the work of the household,"* Ice says in a voice that sounds just like Liddy's. When he sees that Knuckles McGraw's hands are too full of lunch kit to take them, he deals the knives and forks around the table like cards. Very noisy cards.

Joe watches for a moment, then laughs. "Come on. Groundnut stew. Lid, will you get the soda bread out of the oven? Breezy, salad's in the fridge. Everyone sit." He directs Knuckles to a chair at the round table. "This will be your place as long as you're here." Joe looks at the lunch kit still in Knuckles McGraw's hands. "You can put it down," Joe tells him.

Knuckles carefully places it under his chair where he can still feel it with his foot when he sits down.

He hoped there would be beans. Cowboys eat beans and drink coffee with grounds in the bottom that they dump out of their tin mugs when they are done.

"What can I help you to?" Liddy asks him.

He looks at the plate of sliced pickles, laid out in a circle like green tongues. A pile of bread slices topple off a yellow plate. A deep red bowl is full of salad. A wooden board is piled with chunks and rounds of cheese. He takes one piece of cheese and puts it on his plate.

Ice has his elbow stuck way out at the side as he shovels stew noisily into his mouth like a cowboy eating beans from a tin plate. Breezy is sorting her salad into piles. Lettuce in one heap. Sliced carrot and chunks of tomato into another.

Ice looks at him sideways without pulling his head away from his soup. "Our Breezy likes her colors all separate. Come on, man. Grab something to eat. It will be gone soon enough." As he dumps a spoonful of stew into Knuckles McGraw's bowl, some splatters across the red-and-white-checkered tablecloth.

Joe hands Ice a napkin. "We're vegetarian here," he tells Knuckles McGraw. "But we do keep a supply of hot dogs."

"Veggie dogs! Not the same thing," says Ice as he reaches for a slice of bread. He folds it in half and shoves it into his mouth. "If a man wants meat around here, he has to get it at the Turbo Burger. But not tonight," he sneers. "After chores. Chores first. The Turbo Burger later."

"Breezy. Now that's organized, get it eaten, would you?" Liddy says. The silent girl picks up one small piece of salad at a time. She dips it into the dressing on her side plate, then eats it slowly.

Maybe that's how this family will spend the evening, thinks Knuckles McGraw. Eating supper one leaf at a time. Waiting for everyone to be done. Instead of eating a sandwich in front of the TV, or a Pizza Pocket standing at the kitchen counter.

As he digs into his stew with his elbow in the air, just like Ice, Knuckles McGraw wonders what Burlington Northern would eat for supper. And how fast they would have to ride across the plains to escape from this strange family and make it back home before dark.

CHAPTER 5

Cowboys Don't Do Dishes

Knuckles McGraw feels good with his hands in a sink full of soapy water, the warmth creeping up his arms. His fingers make underwater clattery sounds with the cutlery. "We don't have a dishwasher either," he says.

Liddy dumps a stack of plates and bowls at his elbow. "We do have one. But this way we get to visit while the chores get done."

There's only him and Liddy in the kitchen right now. Ice is doing his homework upstairs. Music pounds through the kitchen ceiling. Joe is in the next room helping Breezy with her spelling list. Knuckles McGraw listens hard, but he can't hear her reciting the words. "Doesn't Breezy talk?" he asks.

"Not for a long while." Liddy stands with her back against the counter, watching him sideways as she hands him a dirty bowl.

He swirls it through the water. "Why?"

"We're not sure. The doctors say she could speak if she wanted. There's nothing physical to explain it."

"Maybe she just has nothing to say." When he was Kevin Mason, he sometimes thought people talked too much. His mother was always explaining things to him that he did not want to know about. Why her last boyfriend left. Or what a jerk her boss was, and why she got fired. Teachers talk too much about fractions and other stuff he doesn't get. The more they talk, sometimes the less he gets it. Everything except spelling.

"You may well be right." Liddy is holding his lunch box. "Breezy stopped talking after her parents died. It's not been easy for anyone." She starts to open the first latch on the Wagon Train lunch box.

"No!" As he grabs it from her, water and soap bubbles dribble down his arm and onto the floor. "I'll do that. It's mine."

"Okay."

"I'll do it later." His heart is thumping loudly as he sets it on the counter where she can't reach it. He dunks his hands into the sink again.

"You've probably seen the pictures in the hall." Liddy is busy putting things away. "Those are pictures Breezy drew of her parents. I made the frames. That's what I do. Carpentry. Cabinetry. Anything with wood."

His heart has slowed down a bit. "You are a good frame maker. She's a good drawer."

"I think so too." Liddy wipes a soap dribble off his arm. "I know your mother's note is in your lunch kit," she says gently. "I wonder if we should find a better place for it."

He sticks a handful of knives and forks upside down in the dish rack.

"Somewhere in your room, perhaps?" she asks.

He keeps his hands in the water as he watches Liddy watching him. He thinks of the line down the middle of the bunkhouse. If he has to stick on his own side, does that mean Ice will stay on his? "Somewhere else," he says. "Not the bedroom."

Liddy cleans off the table while he pulls the plug and hears the water gurgle away.

With his back to Liddy, he undoes the latches on his Wagon Train lunch box and pushes back the lid. The notepaper is oily from the peanut butter and sticky from the strawberry jelly. He unwraps it carefully from the sandwich and smoothes it out on the counter, just like Ice did with his iceberg picture.

The writing is still clear. *Please look after my son. I can't take care of him anymore.*

His eyes sting with tears. He used to like peanut butter and jelly. But he won't ever eat it again. He picks up the sandwich and squeezes until the filling oozes onto his fingers. Then he drops the mangled bread into the garbage can.

Part of him wants to scrunch his mother's note up in a tiny ball and throw it in there too. But instead, without reading it again, he folds it once, then again, and slips it in the back pocket of his jeans.

"Remember to take that out before those go in the laundry," Liddy says as she straightens the chairs around the table. Five of them. One each for her and Joe. One for Breezy. One for Ice. And a chair especially for Knuckles McGraw. It's his own place as long as he stays there, Joe told him.

But Knuckles McGraw the cowboy won't need it for long. His mother will get another job, and soon there will be food in the house and the cable TV will get hooked up again so she can watch all her favorite programs.

Breezy's parents are dead. But his mother is just missing. She will come back and get him soon.

But how can he be sure? She's done some strange stuff, lots of times. But she's never left him with a bunch of vegetarians with weird names before. However sick or broke she was. Maybe if Kevin Mason had been a better boy, she would not have left him.

As soon as he has thought it, he tries to un-think it. But it's too late.

"Is Ice your son?" he asks. "Or are you his grandma?"

"Goodness, no," says Liddy. "You could say he is between parents right now." She tidies the salt and pepper and napkins on the table. "His dad can't always take care of him. And he is not always easy for his mom to have around. So he spends time with us. He adds spice to our life, that's for sure." She picks up his lunch box and passes it to him with both hands. Like a present. "This must be very special," she says.

He nods as he takes it from her. But he can't say anything through the thick lump in his throat.

"Did you know it's from an old TV program, *Wagon Train?* I don't think it's been on for years." She hums a snippet of a tune and then asks, "Do you like cowboy shows?"

"Yes," he tells her in a whispery voice. He coughs a little. "I think I might like to be a cowboy. But first I need a horse."

"Well then. You just may be in luck." She snaps off the light and heads out of the kitchen. "Let's go see what your roommate is up to."

CHAPTER 6

Community Service

Ice is lying on his bed. His head and arms hang over the edge as he reads something on the floor. When he sees Knuckles McGraw and Liddy, he shoves it into the shadows and scrambles to his feet. "How about knocking?"

"I'm sorry," says Liddy.

"Forget it," says Ice. "What's up?"

"This young man is interested in horses. I thought you might take him along to the center with you one day. Ice works at the equestrian center," Liddy tells Knuckles McGraw.

"Unpaid work," says Ice. "Hardly counts."

"What do you think?" asks Liddy.

"I have better things to do than hang out with little kids," grumbles Ice. "Bad enough to share a room, like we're brothers or something."

"It doesn't matter," says Knuckles McGraw. There's probably no horse there called Burlington Northern, anyway. Wherever this center is.

"It certainly does matter," Liddy says. "I am asking your roommate to do something for someone else." She bends over and straightens Ice's bedcovers. "I will leave you to discuss logistics. And then we'd enjoy your company downstairs. Breezy should have her homework done by then." She leans toward the pictures above Ice's bed. "I see you have a few new ones." She taps the one he put up earlier. "This is quite lovely. I'll see you both downstairs."

As soon as the door closes, Ice lunges forward and grabs the lunch box from Knuckles McGraw's hand. "What have we got here then?" He waves it high in the air.

"Hey! Give it to me."

Ice shakes it. "It's just a lunch box, for Pete's sake." It rocks back and forth above Knuckles McGraw's head.

"Give it to me. That's mine," he yells. When he jumps up and down, his fingers graze the bottom. But he still can't grab it. "It's private," he says. He reaches for Ice's slippery leather sleeve, but the other boy yanks his arm away. Knuckles McGraw topples across the room. He falls on top of the chalk line separating the two sides of the bunkhouse. "My mom bought me that," he cries. His voice comes in spurts. Between the words are sobs that make his chest hurt. "Give me back my lunch box. It's not yours."

Ice leans forward and drops it onto Knuckles McGraw's bed. "Okay. Okay." He puts up his hands in surrender. "Chill out, man. I was just kidding you. You gotta learn to take a joke."

Knuckles McGraw sits on the edge of his bed and hugs his Wagon Train lunch box to his chest. "It's not funny."

Ice has his back to him, peering at the iceberg pictures as if he has never seen them before. Knuckles McGraw wonders, why does Ice always wear his jacket in the house? Maybe it's as special to Ice as his lunch box is to him. But he is not going to ask him now. If he had his way, he would never speak to this boy again.

Ice flops down onto his bed. He lies back with his arms folded behind his head. "You want to know about my job or not?" he says to the ceiling.

"No!"

"Sure you do."

"I don't."

"Fine. I won't tell you then."

Knuckles McGraw listens to the silence for a bit. Then he says, "Okay. Tell me. But I still think you're mean."

"I knew you'd come around," says Ice.

Knuckles McGraw lies down on his own bed, on top of the covers. He rests the Wagon Train lunch box on his chest so he can keep one hand on it. "What do you do there?" he asks.

"I fetch and carry. Fetch this. Carry that," Ice says. "It's no big deal, for Pete's sake. I muck out stalls. I hose down the stables. Any fool can do it. Any more questions?"

"Tell me their names."

"There's Marilee. She owns the place. And Stu…"

"I mean the horses."

"Oh. The horses," says Ice. "Thunder. Silveree." His bed squeaks, as if he's getting comfortable.

"He's a handful. You gotta watch out for him. Caleb. Fantasia. Lily. She's a sweetie. I'll ride her one day. Adelina…"

Knuckles McGraw leans over his bed and pushes his lunch box underneath as far back and as quietly as he can. Just like Ice shoved whatever he was reading out of sight. Then he rolls back into the middle of his bed and pulls the blankets up to his middle.

Ice is still reciting names. "Sugarloaf. Island Breeze. He's new. Don't know about him yet. Showgirl. Price is Right…"

The words start to drift away, as if each name is creeping through the door and down the stairs almost as soon as Ice says it. Knuckles McGraw the cowboy tries to stay awake. In case there is another horse called Burlington Northern. But his eyes grow heavier and heavier. And slowly the room fades away, along with all the horses that clatter past in his dreams, each one with a cowboy on its back.

CHAPTER 7

Curfew

When Knuckles McGraw wakes up, the room is full of silvery light. He lies shivering for a minute and then sits up on the edge of the bed.

Ice has gone. He hears the rumble of a TV from downstairs and the murmur of voices rising through the floor. He pulls up his knees and wraps his arms around them. But he is still cold.

Suddenly he realizes that he has no pajamas, or toothpaste. A cowboy would have a saddlebag with blankets and one change of clothes. Some soap maybe. But Knuckles McGraw only has a Wagon Train lunch box and a greasy note in his pocket.

He gets up and goes downstairs, where Breezy is standing on her head in one corner of the living room with her bare feet propped against the wall. Joe puts his book on the table next to his chair when Knuckles McGraw comes in. "There you are. We were wondering if we should wake you up."

"I don't have any pajamas."

"We can soon fix that." With Breezy following, Joe leads him to a big cupboard in the hall. Inside are stacks of jeans and sweaters, a basket of socks, one of underwear. And a heap of pajamas that Joe lifts down from the high shelf and drops into Knuckles McGraw's hands. "There you go. There should be at least one pair that fits."

Breezy shuffles through the heap of pajamas Knuckles McGraw is holding and pulls out a blue-and-white-striped pair. She pushes them at his chest.

"I can choose my own," he says.

She shakes them in front of his face.

"Okay. Okay. I don't care." He dumps the rest back on a shelf and takes the pair she wants him to have. "It might help if you talked sometimes."

She sticks out her tongue and walks away.

He is wondering whether to go back upstairs or into the living room, when Ice creeps into the house.

He closes the front door quietly and puts one finger across his lips when he sees Knuckles McGraw.

"What time is it?" asks Joe, coming up behind Ice.

Ice shoves his sleeve up and looks at his bare wrist where a watch should be. "Beats me," he says.

"We have curfew in this house," says Joe. "As you well know."

"It got away from me."

"That's not good enough. We ask for you to be home at nine." Joe shoves his fingers into the front pockets of his jeans and stands watching Ice. "What can you do to make up for your tardiness?"

"Tardiness!" Ice's voice is hard and thin.

Knuckles McGraw wishes his horse was tied nearby. He'd grab his reins and jump onto his back and ride right out of here. Joe's and Ice's angry voices rattle back and forth like Ping-Pong balls flickering across a table. With him in the middle. He looks at one of them, then the other. He sees their mouths moving. Ice's cheeks get red. Joe shifts from one foot to the other as their voices get louder and louder.

Suddenly, Liddy's voice cuts through the roaring noise that fills Knuckles McGraw's head.

"That's enough. You're upsetting the boy. Come on." She takes his hand, and he lets her. "Let's head upstairs," she says. "Breezy is off to bed too." Liddy's hair is even more full of sawdust now. And it's all over her shoulders. "Let's not upset our guest on his first night with us."

He looks at the changing pictures on the wall as he climbs the stairs. The woman's eyes are the same color as Breezy's.

When he reaches the top, Breezy is coming out of the bathroom in her pajamas. They are exactly like the ones she made him take from the pile in the cupboard.

They will look just like twins!

CHAPTER 8

Secret and Private

Ice is just a big lump under the covers when Knuckles McGraw wakes up the next morning. And he's still there the third time Knuckles McGraw heads to the bathroom. If he was a cowboy, he could go for a pee behind a tree. Or out back of the saloon. A cowboy on the range would not have to worry about waiting for other people to use the bathroom first.

Breezy pokes her head out of her room. She disappears again when she sees him.

What if he pees his new blue pajamas waiting for his turn?

He is about to knock on the bathroom door when Liddy comes out. Her hair sticks up in little spikes, like Ice's. Her face is pink and damp. "One day we'll get around to putting in another bathroom," she tells him. "Go ahead."

He washes his face with a green and white facecloth. A smudgy glass on the sink is full of toothbrushes. But they all have bent bristles and toothpaste on their handles. So he scrubs his teeth with his finger.

If he stays here long enough, maybe he'll have his own new toothbrush and another pair of pajamas for when these go in the wash. New school clothes, maybe. Toys on his birthday and a bulging stocking at Christmas.

For a minute the idea of having his own stuff at Liddy and Joe's feels good. Then he thinks about rules and after-school chores. A curfew like Ice's.

Lots of kids have bedtimes. And chores. When he's Kevin Mason, his mom lets him do pretty well anything when she's around. And when she isn't, he can still do anything, as long as he does not use the stove or make long-distance phone calls.

When he comes out of the bathroom, Breezy is sitting on the floor beside the door. She follows him into his room and thumps down onto Ice's bed. He sticks his head out of the covers, like a turtle looking out of its shell. "Get lost, kid," he growls at Breezy.

She steps carefully over the chalk line on the carpet and walks over to Knuckles McGraw's bed and climbs onto it. She does a headstand with her feet propped against the wall. When her pajama top slips down, showing her purple undershirt, she grabs it with one hand. She tips sideways, topples over and lands on the carpet with a thump.

"Are you all right?" he asks. She sits in a lump on the floor, hiding her face in her arms. "Should I get Liddy?" he asks. "Ice? Should I get Liddy?"

But Ice's bed is empty.

Knuckles McGraw pats Breezy's arm, then her back. She is making little mewing noises like a lost kitten would make. Or a dog who wants to be let out.

He thinks he hears her say *Ow. Ow. Ow.* He leans closer and says, "Did you say something? Are you okay? Did you say something?"

She pulls her head up and frowns at him. Her whole face is blotchy and white.

Can she really talk, and is she silent all the time because she really doesn't have anything to say? Except "Ow" when she gets hurt? Did he imagine it? Or has Breezy let out a secret by mistake?

"Kevin! Breezy! Get a move on. Ice!" Joe calls up the stairs.

Knuckles McGraw is hungry. He didn't eat much at supper last night. Anyway, Liddy says he's a guest. And guests have to fit in. That's what his mom told him when they went to stay with one of her boyfriends in Langley. Then they left him for a whole day while they went for a drive into the valley without him.

"It's breakfast time," he tells Breezy. She is just sniffling now. Maybe he just imagined that he heard her speak. "I have to get dressed," he tells her. "Don't you?"

When he gets a horse called Burlington Northern, Knuckles McGraw can eat his breakfast over a campfire if he wants to. But maybe today Liddy and Joe have waffles.

Very slowly, Breezy gets up and tugs her pajama top down tight. Then she trots out of the room without looking back.

CHAPTER 9

Family Matters

All through breakfast, Knuckles McGraw doesn't say a word except "Please" and "Thank you" to eggs and toast and a bowl of applesauce. Joe makes sandwiches at the counter, while Liddy reads the paper at the table. Ice shovels food just like he did last night, with one elbow stuck out like a wing.

Breezy watches Knuckles McGraw under her eyebrows the whole time. Sometimes she frowns, like she's warning him to keep her secret quiet. So he does. Who would he tell? And what would he tell them?

Secrets are sticky things. One minute it feels good to keep them. The next minute it seems a good idea to give them away, like something that's too heavy to carry.

Liddy snaps her paper closed. "Joe will drop off Ice and Breeze. Kev…Knuckles McGraw, you don't need to go to school today. I'll explain later."

He scoops up the last dribble of applesauce and eats the crust of his toast.

Joe holds up two paper-bag lunches. "Let's go, guys."

Breezy kisses Liddy's cheek. Ice follows Joe and Breezy through the back door without even saying goodbye. He's wearing different jeans today. These have writing down them too. His name scrawled over and over again in all kinds of writing. *ICE ICE ICE ICE ICE.*

Knuckles McGraw wears the same pants and shirt as yesterday. Maybe he will write his name, and Burlington Northern's, down his jeans later. Maybe Ice will lend him his silver marker.

He is just finishing clearing the table for Liddy when he hears a car pull up outside. He dashes to the door and throws it open.

But it's only the welfare lady again.

"Am I going home now?" he asks.

Liddy stands behind him, with one hand on his shoulder. "Just for a bit," she says.

He grabs his lunch box from under his seat at the table.

"You can leave that here," Liddy tells him. "Ms. Havers is just taking you to pick up a few things you need for the next little while."

The welfare lady is wearing colorful parrot earrings that swing against her collar. His mom has some almost like them.

He feels the crinkly feeling around his ears that means he might cry. But he's a cowboy. And cowboys don't cry. He swallows hard, "Will my mom be there?"

"I don't think so," says Ms. Havers. "But we need you to show us where she keeps her address book. Or letters maybe. So we can track down your family."

"There's only me and Mom. And my dad…" He looks down at his feet and grips the handle of his lunch box tight.

Kevin Mason's mother calls his dad TM, which she once told him stands for Tragic Mistake. One day he sat down and looked through all the TMs in the phone book. Then he filled up the two lined pages at the back with the names that could be his father's. *Tanjit Mann. Tony Miller. Troy Minnow. Ted Mission. Trevor Montgomery.* There were lots of them.

When his mother found the list, she ripped the pages out.

If he did have a father, wouldn't he have been there to pick him up from school after his mom put a note in his lunch box saying that she could not look after him?

Suddenly, he remembers something. There was a man whose wide-brimmed hat hid his eyes. Who sang cowboy songs. Who let Kevin Mason sit on his back as he trotted around the room like a horse until he fell off. Way back before he was Knuckles McGraw, the cowboy who would like to roam the range under the big sky. "I forgot. But I know now!" he tells Ms. Havers and Liddy. "I think my dad is a rodeo rider!"

That's not quite what he meant to say. But it makes sense, doesn't it? A rodeo rider can't stay home to make sure his kid is taken care of and that the kid's mother keeps a job and makes meals and is there when her boy comes home from school.

"I don't think so," says Ms. Havers.

Knuckles McGraw feels a huge wave of anger surge through him. It's like the molten lava he learned about in school when they were studying volcanoes.

It is heavy and thick, and he knows it cannot be stopped once it has started.

He is the one whose mom left him that note in his lunch box. *He* is the one whose dad lassoes cows and rides bucking horses bareback and sleeps under the big sky with the campfire roaring beside him.

How does this lady with the silly bird earrings know what it feels like to be stuck in this peculiar house with a girl who can't talk but does, and a boy with a stupid name, and a grandma who is always covered in sawdust and a grandpa who has a ponytail? How would this lady feel if she did not know where *her* mother was or if she will ever come home? How can she know more about his own dad than he does? "Listen to me, why don't you?" he yells.

The welfare lady's face puckers up into a frown. Liddy is looking at him through wide eyes. He can see a fleck of brown sawdust on her eyelash.

And he remembers something else! His mom's parents in Edmonton used to call. And sometimes his mom cried and sometimes she yelled. And often what she yelled was, "Listen to me, why don't you?" And then she'd yell some more into the phone very fast, without giving her mom or dad, or his grandma and grandpa or whoever they were, a chance to answer.

Knuckles McGraw says it again, but not quite shouting this time because he feels all out of breath with remembering: "Listen to me, why don't you?"

Liddy and the welfare lady stand watching him. They look at each other and back at him.

But now he has nothing to say. The man in the cowboy hat could have been anyone. It could have been any of his mom's boyfriends. He has never been to Edmonton and doesn't remember if he ever met his grandparents. And no one knows where his mom is, or why she left him.

Not even the welfare lady, who acts like she knows everything.

He is suddenly cold all over and shivering. The two ladies look all shimmery through his tears.

The welfare lady stands with one hand on the doorknob. Liddy has her arms out to him. She speaks very quietly. "Come here," she says.

And so he does. He takes two steps. He moves around the table, away from the welfare lady. And he lets himself be pulled gently into Breezy's grandma's arms.

CHAPTER 10

Mixed-up Memories

Knuckles McGraw washes his face with cold water, but it still feels hot from all the tears he cried into Liddy's shoulder. She smelled of wood shavings and soap.

He's in the welfare lady's car again now. They want him to help find some information about his family. They told him he can bring back his own pajamas and toothbrush and more clothes. And anything else that is important to him.

When he sniffs, Ms. Havers roots in the glove compartment and hands him a creased tissue. "We'll be back before lunch," she tells him.

"My mom has earrings like that," he tells her. "But the parrots are purple."

She touches one, where it dangles against her neck. "I forgot I was wearing them." She laughs. "They are a gift from a little girl called Janine, who I see once in a while. She bought them for my birthday. Nice, aren't they?"

"Happy birthday."

"It's not for another few months. She gave them to me now in case she forgets." When she laughs again, her voice is like a tinkling bell. For the first time, Knuckles McGraw likes this lady who has promised to bring him right back to Liddy and Joe's if his mom is not home yet.

Soon they are both standing before his front door. Prem, the building manager says, "I am not sure about this."

Ms. Havers shows him a paper.

"Very well." Prem unlocks the door. "But I will be staying with you."

Knuckles McGraw looks at the little gold stool outside the door, with the dead plant in a flowerpot on top of it. But he doesn't move a finger toward it. He is the only one who knows where the key is kept so he can get inside when his mom's not home.

Walking in past Prem, who waits outside the front door, Knuckles McGraw remembers what it felt like to be Kevin Mason in his empty house. He walks quickly down the dark hallway. He peeks into his own room. He stops for a moment outside his mom's room, but doesn't go in.

The living room has no door. It's empty and dark too. The kitchen looks just like it did when he saw it last. His breakfast dishes are still on the table next to the magazine his mom was reading while he ate. "She's not here." He pokes his finger into a shiny circle of dried milk on the table.

"I know, Kevin," says Ms. Havers. She touches his back. "We have been calling. The machine picks up every time."

The answering machine light is flickering 5 off and on. "Maybe she called," he says. He leans over and pushes the Play button. On the machine, Ms. Havers's voice says almost the same thing over and over. "Ms. Mason? We need to locate you so we can reunite you with your son. Or find out how we can support your family. Please call us." Then she recites her phone number.

By the time he's heard the fifth message that always says the same thing, Knuckles McGraw knows he will remember Ms. Havers's number forever.

She is busy poking through the kitchen drawers. She peers at the notes and pictures on the fridge. "Where does your mother keep special papers?" she asks.

"In the coffee table." He leads her into the living room. In the drawer under the table is a pack of cards and a jigsaw puzzle in a box with a broken lid. He pulls out three old *TV Guides* and some school newsletters that he can't remember bringing home. Underneath he finds his mother's blue address book. "Maybe my dad's address is in here." He hands it to Ms. Havers.

"Perhaps your grandparents' too." She opens it up.

"They live in Edmonton, where the Oilers come from."

"I bet your grandfather is a fan," she says.

"I've never met him," he says.

Ms. Havers flips through the book. She asks him about some names. But the only ones he knows are Dr. King and Sue Draper, who his mom used to go to movies with. Then she turns to another page and asks, "How about Lyle and Gloria Mason?"

"Maybe that's them," he tells her. "They have the same last name as me and my mom."

"This is a good start." Ms. Havers tucks the little book into her purse. "Now, how about we go and find some clothes to take back to Liddy's. A favorite toy or two?"

"I can do it."

"Go and get what you need, then. Don't forget socks and underwear. I'll look for something to put them in. Does your mom have a suitcase?"

"Under her bed."

When he comes out of his room with his arms full of clothes and his Lego space station balanced on the top of the pile, a black plastic garbage bag is sitting on the coffee table. "No suitcase," says Ms. Havers. "I expect she has it with her. This will do." She takes the clothes he hands her, then folds everything tidily back into the bag. "What about pj's?"

"Joe gave me new ones."

"Are we all set then?"

He looks around. At the dark gray screen of the TV and the tall ashtray on a pole that holds a wrinkly old houseplant. At the row of paperbacks on the shelf under the window.

He is about to follow Ms. Havers out of the room when he grabs a picture from the shelf and shoves it under his arm. He'll put the picture into his lunch box just as soon as he gets outside.

The photo was taken years ago, when he was just four, sitting in the train at Bear Creek Park. His mom is looking at something else while he grins into the camera. Ice cream is smeared around his mouth. He remembers it was chocolate.

But maybe it's just another mixed-up memory. Like the one of riding around on the back of a man who sang cowboy songs that Knuckles McGraw can no longer remember.

CHAPTER 11

Sound and Fury

Ms. Havers buys McDonald's for lunch. She even asks if it comes with a little toy. But there's no special deal on, so Knuckles McGraw has to make do with chicken nuggets and fries.

She orders a box of nine nuggets. "I'll share one or two with you, if I may," she tells him.

The box sits on his lap, making his legs warm. The car starts to smell chickeny. They stop at the same park where he went on the train when he was little. But now, in the rain, there's only one other person in the parking lot, reading a book in his car and munching a very large apple.

Knuckles McGraw and Ms. Havers stay where they are with the radio on quietly in the background.

He eats without talking while she nibbles one piece of chicken. "Fries aren't good for my waistline," she tells him when he offers her one.

When he's eaten four pieces of chicken and all the fries, he wipes his mouth and rattles the bag to see if there are any left in the bottom.

The man in the other car is still reading. He's eating his apple core now.

Knuckles McGraw looks around for the little train he went on when he was still Kevin Mason. But all he can see is rain dribbling down the window and hazy trees in the distance. "What will you say if you call my grandparents?" he asks.

"Well, I'll ask if they've heard from your mom." She wipes her mouth with a napkin. "If they have, I'll try and track her down. But I may need to find out if they are willing to take care of you until she comes home."

"They live in Edmonton."

"That's a long way away, I know. You'd miss your friends."

"Not really. Andrew was my friend at the last school. But then we came here."

"Who do you play with now?"

At this school, where he's only been for a while, his teacher sometimes pairs him with Simon Galway or Amar Dhaliwal. But they aren't friends. "Just Ice and Breezy, I guess," he tells her.

She turns sideways to look at him. "How are you getting on at Liddy's?"

"Okay. But they are weird. Breezy doesn't talk much. I mean"—he goes on quickly before she can notice the secret he almost gave away—"Ice is okay. It's a funny name."

"Oh yes, Ice. Is he friendly?"

"Sometimes. But sometimes he gets mad at me."

"All sound and fury signifying nothing," says Ms. Havers. "That's from Shakespeare. But it applies to our friend. He wouldn't hurt a fly. He's just one unhappy boy. But I hear he likes you. Give him time, and he'll melt a bit."

Just like an iceberg, thinks Knuckles McGraw.

Ms. Havers hands him a napkin as she finishes his last chicken piece. "You've got ketchup on your cheek."

He feels something warm inside him. "Ice likes me?"

"Sure he does. Now. If you're done, I can get you back to Liddy's. Or would you rather go to school this afternoon?"

"School."

Ms. Havers starts the car, but they don't go anywhere. Instead, she turns to look at him. "Here's what's going to happen."

He is still thinking about Ice. He likes him! It is not always easy to tell.

"Kevin. You with me?" Ms. Havers taps his knee.

"My name is Knuckles McGraw now."

"Knuckles, then."

Why doesn't anyone get it? It only sounds right when the names are together. But she's still talking, so he doesn't interrupt.

"If we can't trace your mother, we will try your grandparents," says Ms. Havers. "If they are willing to have you—even if it's just for a while until we find your mom—you will go to Edmonton to be with them. But if not, we would have to make a more formal agreement for your care."

"Can't I stay at Liddy and Joe's?"

"That's the other option."

"I like that better." The other car is leaving now, sending up a cloud of gray smoke as it goes. It probably needs a tune-up. A horse called Burlington Northern would never need a tune-up. But he might need a warm stable from time to time.

"How about we see what happens with your grandma and grandpa?" says Ms. Havers.

"I don't know them."

"You didn't know Liddy and Joe. Nor Ice and Breezy until yesterday."

"I want to go home." He kicks at the chicken box and the chip bag on the floor. It rattles with a chip in the bottom he must have missed.

"You can't go home alone, Kevin. I'm sure you know that."

"If I can't go home, I will run away. Cowboys can live out on the range for days," he says, staring at the glove compartment. "For months, even. Knuckles McGraw is a cowboy." He almost tells her about Burlington Northern. But it's private. He's going to keep his horse's name a secret for now. "And my name is *not* Kevin Mason anymore," he yells.

He grabs the door handle and tugs at it. But it is one of those cars that can lock a person in. All he wants to do is take off on his horse across the open plains until the night falls and it's time to make camp under the glittery stars.

CHAPTER 12

Horses Close Up

When she has Knuckles McGraw trapped in the car, Ms. Havers talks and talks for a long time while he watches the rain blow harder and harder against the windshield until all he can see is a gray curtain of water. She finally runs out of things to say and sits still, as if she is waiting for him to answer some of her questions.

But all he says is, "I want to go to school now."

She drives in silence and only speaks again when they get there. "Joe will be here at two thirty to pick up you and Breezy. He'll meet you right here."

Knuckles McGraw slams the door and walks away without answering.

Everyone is just settling into their desks after lunch when he gets there. Luckily, he missed math this morning. He's way ahead reading *White Jade Tiger*, so he spends his spare time learning new words from the dictionary, like he always does.

Equestrian backward is N-A-I-R-T-S-E-U-Q-E. Now he knows that the place Ice works at trains horses. G-R-E-B-E-C-I. *Iceberg* looks funny spelled that way. W-A-R-G-C-M-S-E-L-K-C-U-N-K. *Knuckles McGraw* spelled backward is too hard to say.

Joe is waiting in his truck at the curb when school lets out. He helps Breezy up, then waits until Knuckles McGraw is in before he starts the engine. "We're going on an outing," he tells them as he pulls into traffic.

Knuckles McGraw sits with his face pressed against the window as they drive along streets he knows. After they pass the Walmart, they are in another world of big fields and white fences. On one side of the road, he sees a hut with a sign advertising eggs for sale. *Free Range*, it says. Even chickens get to go out on the range. They'd better be careful they don't get stomped on by horses like Price is Right or Burlington Northern.

Joe listens to the radio. Breezy keeps her head bent as she draws in her school binder. She tears out each page when she finishes it and shoves it into her schoolbag. When he tries to look over her arm, she shields the page with her body so he can't see. Whatever he says to her, she just nods or blinks. But she doesn't say a word.

If she really said "Ow" this morning, it must be a big secret.

The truck jounces down a bumpy road between fields and long fences. On one side are horses. Some are wearing blankets. Their long necks are stretched down to the ground, their manes flowing over their shoulders. They all look happy enough, but it doesn't seem fair that some get coats and others don't.

"We're here." Joe pulls up in front of a big building with a wide-open front.

Knuckles McGraw stands waiting beside the truck door while Breezy jumps down and runs into the darkness of the barn.

"Let's surprise Ice," says Joe, leading the way. Inside, the building smells of wet straw, mud and what might be pee. It is steamy and cold at the same time, and Knuckles McGraw hears shoving and sighing all around.

As his eyes get used to the darkness, he can make out horses sticking their heads over the stall doors. He walks down the middle of the echoing cement corridor. Up ahead, Ice's jacket chains rattle as he heaves great piles of straw on the end of a long fork.

"How's this for a surprise?" Joe says to Ice. "Thought we could give you a ride home."

"I'm getting one with Marilee." Ice does not look pleased to see them. His cheek is smudged with dirt, and straw sticks out of one of his boots.

"How about you show Knuckles McGraw around?" asks Joe.

"Breeze can do it as well as me," says Ice. "Can't you see I'm busy?"

The nearest horse nickers and fidgets. When its hooves clatter on the ground, Knuckles McGraw steps back, right up against the next stall. The horse inside tosses its head and blows hot breath against his ear.

He jumps away.

"Not scared of horses, are you?" Ice jeers. He opens the door and pushes past the horse's gleaming side into the stall.

"Am not!" says Knuckles McGraw. But he feels sweaty and out of breath. There's no safe place to stand.

Joe puts a hand on his shoulder. "They seem twice as big close up, don't they?"

"Coming through," says Ice. "Gotta get this big boy out of here so I can do some housecleaning."

Knuckles McGraw stands close to Joe as Ice leads a big brown horse down the aisle and into an empty stall at the end. His face is next to the horse's, whispering to it as he leads it along. He even kisses its bulgy cheek.

"Where did Breezy get to?" Joe heads deeper into the barn, with Knuckles McGraw following close behind. On both sides of the aisle, horses shift and whinny, staring at Knuckles McGraw with their glossy dark eyes. They blink their long eyelashes, then toss their heads, banging them against the wooden walls and doors.

Breezy is sitting on the ground with two kittens in her lap. She looks up at Joe with a begging look on her face. He seems to know what she's asking, even though she doesn't say a word. "We've had this conversation before, Breeze." He bends down and scratches one of the cats behind its ears. "I wouldn't mind at all. But your grandma has allergies." He picks up the other cat and holds it right in front of his face, looking into its eyes as its body dangles from his hands. "Put this in the same room as Liddy, and she'll be in agony. But this is a cutie, for sure."

Breezy stands up and thrusts a cat into Knuckles McGraw's hands. He buries his face in its soft tummy fur.

"Come on, guys." Joe puts his kitten back in a pile of straw and walks back the way they came. Knuckles McGraw's kitten dances away in a crooked line. He hopes it stays out of the way of horse hooves.

Joe strides ahead. "Let's say goodbye to Ice." Breezy makes a sulky face as she drags her feet and follows, slapping the stalls as she passes each one.

Knuckles McGraw is careful to stay out of reach of the horses on his way back to the truck. He's nervous around these ones.

But Burlington Northern is nothing to be scared of.

CHAPTER 13

Just to Say Hello

Knuckles McGraw gets used to the routine at Joe and Liddy's. And the rules. No cartoons in the morning. TV only after supper and homework. Everyone contributes to the "work of the household," as Liddy calls it. Joe makes supper. Liddy comes in from her woodworking and sets the table. Knuckles McGraw does dishes while Breezy does handstands against the wall. Then she dries.

Ice puts out the garbage and sorts the recycling. He makes a racket doing it, complaining loudly that he has a real job, and he shouldn't have to do chores.

Knuckles McGraw likes it that he knows what to expect each morning when he gets up, and every day after school. Sometimes it's like everything is fine, just for now. Then he worries about what will happen next.

The Monday after his first weekend without his mom, Joe picks Breezy and him up from school, as usual. But when they're in the truck, he says, "Breeze, I'm dropping you off at Jean's. She's a family friend," he tells Knuckles McGraw. "A grown-up foster kid who was with us off and on for years."

Knuckles McGraw fiddles with the radio until he finds the country station with twangy guitar music. On the way to school, Ice gets to choose the music. It's always loud. On the way home, Breezy and Knuckles McGraw take turns.

Maybe one day he will get a guitar. A guitar would be a good thing for a cowboy to have out on the range on the lonely nights when it's just him and his trusty horse sleeping under the stars.

Jean lives in a suite in a big house with washing hanging over all the fences and on the big deck upstairs. He watches the clothes flap as she and Breezy disappear through the front door.

"We have visitors," Joe says, as he waits to pulls away into traffic. "Thought we might like the house to ourselves for a while." An ambulance races past with its lights flashing.

"Is it my mom?"

"No, I'm afraid it's not your mom. Your grand-parents have come to visit."

"From Edmonton?"

"All this way to see you."

"I've never met them."

"I believe you have," says Joe. But not in the way adults say stuff because they like to think they are right. He says it as if he really does know. "Your grandpa says you were probably about two," Joe continues. "But we'll let him and your grandma tell you all about it."

"Do I have to go to Edmonton with them?" asks Knuckles McGraw. He holds on tight to the handle of his lunch kit while he waits for the answer.

"How about we cross that bridge when we come to it," says Joe. "Think of this as just a chance to say hello."

"Are they nice?"

"They seem to be. But I only met them for ten minutes. They called yesterday, after Ms. Havers got in touch with them. They flew in today."

"I've never been in a plane."

"I bet you'd get to go up in one if you visited your grandparents," Joe says. "It's a long drive to Edmonton."

A big red car is parked outside the house. "I thought you said they flew," says Knuckles McGraw.

"They rented a car at the airport. I'd have picked them up, but they wanted to do it their way. You coming?" Joe opens the passenger door. "Need a hand, partner?"

Knuckles McGraw's legs don't want to move. "Can I come in a minute?"

"You're not going to run away on us, are you?" says Joe.

"No."

"Fine, then. But don't be too long. Liddy's giving them a cup of tea while they wait for you."

"I'll be right in."

"Good show." Joe slaps the side of the truck as he walks away. As if it's a horse that needs settling.

CHAPTER 14

All the Way from Edmonton

The man who gets up from the couch is tall, with a big round stomach under a tight blue denim shirt. "Here's our boy," he says. "I'd have recognized him anywhere." His bald head shines like a big egg.

"Don't be silly, Lyle." A woman with bright red curls and lots of lipstick puts down her cup. "Don't listen to him," she tells Knuckles McGraw. "It has been a long time since we saw you. You're very tall for…eight, isn't it?"

"I'm nine soon."

"January seventh," says the man. "It's on our calendar."

"We're so pleased to see you." His grandmother reaches out to pull him close. She jangles when she moves her arms, which are covered with thin gold brace-lets. "I hope you're not too old for hugs." She smells like shampoo and perfume. Maybe she dressed up just to meet Kevin Mason. Like he's someone special.

"Shall I bring a fresh pot?" Liddy gets up and stands at the door.

"We're fine, I think," says the lady. "We'd just like a chance to visit with our grandson awhile. How does that suit you, Kevin?"

"I'm sure it suits him just fine," says Lyle. He rubs his big stomach. "Maybe we'll take this young man out for a bite of supper in a bit."

When they are alone, the lady—his grandma—rubs her arms as if they are cold. Her noisy bracelets sound like a horse's bridle. "You going to sit down, Lyle?" she asks his grandpa.

For a minute, Knuckles McGraw worries that the man is too big for the chair. But he manages to fit. His stomach rests on his lap like a big blue basketball.

The woman reaches over and pats the man's hand. Then she smiles at Knuckles McGraw. "How about you tell us all about yourself? There's a lot to catch up on."

"I'm waiting for my mom to come back and get me. Did she call you?"

His grandparents look at each other, then back at him. "She didn't, son," says his grandpa. "But she will. She will. She always has, sooner or later. Hasn't she, Gloria?"

"Sooner or later." Her voice is sad. "Your mom and us…well, we don't always seem to get along. It's been difficult."

"But we've always managed to keep in touch somehow, haven't we, Gloria?" asks his grandpa. "Did you want a snack, Kevin?" he asks. "Liddy—isn't she a nice lady?—she supplied us with more cookies than we could possibly eat."

His grandmother pushes the plate along the coffee table toward Knuckles McGraw.

He takes just one. "We made these," he says.

"Get away!" says Lyle. "You planning to be a chef, maybe?"

"I was just helping. Liddy and Breezy did most of the work."

"Now that's an unusual name. I expect you know how your friend got it."

Is Breezy his friend? He doesn't think so. "No." Now that he's used to her, he doesn't think about it. "How?"

"Every little breeze seems to whisper 'Louise,'" sings Gloria. Her voice is light and quavery. "One of my favorites."

"Bet you didn't know your grandma was a singer in her time," says his grandpa. "Her voice still gives me a little flutter. She's a fine dancer too. Square dancing. And she has the flouncy skirts to prove it!"

"Oh, go on." When Gloria gives Lyle's arm a little slap, her painted nails shine.

"Breezy is really Louise?" asks Knuckles McGraw. It's not right that these people know more about her than he does. He and Breezy and Ice are almost like family now. He should know this stuff.

His grandfather leans toward him. "Liddy? Is that her name? She told us a bit about your Breezy. We understand you go by an alias too."

"A what?"

"A name you'd rather be called. Knuckles McGee, is it?"

"McGraw. Knuckles McGraw," he tells them. "They go together."

"And how did you come by that?" His grandmother passes the cookie plate again. There's only one left, so he shakes his head.

"It's a cowboy name. If I was a cowboy, I'd be called Knuckles McGraw. Sometimes I pretend I am a cowboy." He stops before he gives away all his secrets. Or maybe Burlington Northern's name is not quite a secret. But it's private. It's easy to get secrets and private stuff mixed up.

"I've certainly heard stranger names," says Lyle.

"Are there any cowboys in Edmonton?" asks Knuckles McGraw.

"I'd say. A wild lot they are too. Especially when they get together," says his grandma. She has a funny look on her face. The kind of smile adults sometimes have when they are trying to hide something. "You ever met a real cowboy?"

"Not yet."

His grandfather laughs and slaps his leg with his meaty hand. "Well, I'm sure we can fix that. Half the fellows I know are cowboys one way or another."

Knuckles McGraw thinks of all the questions he'd ask them. Where do you go to buy a lasso? How many changes of clothes do you need when you're out riding the range? How does a horse stay warm at night?

Then he remembers the breathless feeling he got when he was surrounded by horses, all staring at him over their stalls. How tall they all were. Like walls that you'd bounce off if you banged up against them.

"I think I should stay here," he says.

His grandmother makes a little mewing noise like Breezy did when she fell off his bed. It sounds like one of the kittens in the barn. When she reaches out and clutches his grandfather's arm, he pats her hand with his big beefy one. "How about you think about it for a while?" he says. "No need to make your mind up right way. Is there, Gloria?"

She swallows. She puts a smile across her mouth, but it's the kind that makes it look like she might cry any minute. "We do hope you'll change your mind."

"You don't even know me," says Knuckles McGraw. "Maybe I still wet my bed. You don't even know if I can do math or if I get bad report cards. Maybe I have bad manners and don't like the food they have in Edmonton." Suddenly he can think of a million reasons that he should not go home with Lyle and Gloria Mason. Even if they are his family. "Maybe I want to stay here with Breezy and Ice. Ice and I share a room. Like brothers. And I think maybe one day I can get Breezy to talk."

"Wouldn't that be just the ticket, if she did!" His grandfather gets up and stands in front of the window, looking out. His back is big and wide. He wears jeans and a wide leather belt. And cowboy boots.

"Where did you get your boots?" Knuckles McGraw asks.

His grandmother answers. "At a tack shop. You'll find all kinds of cowboy boots in Alberta."

"I bet we could find the perfect pair to fit you," says his grandfather. He walks slowly across the room looking down at his feet, then across at Knuckles McGraw's blue runners.

Everyone is quiet for a bit. His grandmother moves her cup on the table, but doesn't pick it up. His grandfather tucks in his shirt, which is already tucked in tight.

"I can't go home with you," Knuckles McGraw tells them. "If I am in Edmonton, how will my mom find me? I need to stay here." He hears voices in the kitchen: Joe and Liddy. Ice's music booms overhead.

"It was nice to meet you," he says. But he doesn't really mean it. He wants to stay here, where he is just getting used to things.

But these two people are his real family. Even a cowboy needs a proper family. It's all so confusing. It's all his mom's fault. If she hadn't gone and left him with just a sticky note in a stupid lunch box from an old TV show that they don't even have on anymore, he wouldn't have to decide whether to stay here or go to Edmonton.

Or whether to be Knuckles McGraw or Kevin Mason.

CHAPTER 15

A Brave Dude

Ice is sitting on the floor looking at a thick black binder when Knuckles McGraw comes upstairs and into their room. He looks up to ask, "And how was the family reunion?"

Instead of answering, Knuckles McGraw stands at the window waiting for his grandma and grandpa to leave in their big red car. His grandma looks up at the house as she gets in, but he does not wave to her.

He sits on his bed and opens his lunch box to make sure his mom's note and the picture of them on the Bear Creek Park train are still there.

"What's so interesting about that dumb box, anyway?" asks Ice.

"It's private," Knuckles McGraw tells him. "Don't you have anything secret?"

Ice rests his elbows on the black binder in his lap. "Secret and private are the same thing. Don't you think?"

This feels like a trick question. His letter from his mom is private. But Liddy knows about it, and the principal and his teacher by now. Maybe all the kids in his class. So it's not quite a secret.

"You got an answer to that?" asks Ice.

"Maybe not." Knuckles McGraw unlatches his lunch kit. Then he locks it again. "Do you have a secret?" he asks Ice again.

"I'm not an ax murderer in my spare time, if that's what you mean." Ice laughs. "But there are lots of little old ladies on the street who cross to the other side when they see me coming." He slaps his binder against his leg, then shoves it in the drawer of his night table. "Not that I care." He pats the top of the table. "But this is private. My stuff in here. You know it's here now, so it can't be a secret. But stay away from it."

"What is it?"

"How about I tell you this much? Just between you and me. It's a study I have been doing. A serious study. It might be my life's work," Ice says importantly. "Or it might just be a waste of time. But it's private. So that's all I need to tell you. Now. Will you R-E-C-I-P-R-O-C-A-T-E? That's the question."

"You have to do it backward," Knuckles McGraw tells him. "It's E-T-A-C-O-R-P-I-C-E-R."

"Whatever, man. So, you going to tell me what's in your lunch box?"

"It's a note from my mom."

"Oh." Ice looks like he's sorry he asked.

Knuckles McGraw thinks about the difference between private and secret. And right here and now, he decides to reciprocate. He will trade his private information for the secret Ice shared with him, even if it wasn't much. It seems fair. "My mom left me a note saying that she could not take care of me instead of picking me up from school that's why I am here." It's not so hard if he says it in a rush.

"Harsh, man. Wow. You are some brave dude. She really say that?"

"Yes." He fiddles with the latches.

"She say why?" asks Ice gently.

Knuckles McGraw shakes his head.

"Oh, man. Parents, hey?" Ice starts to laugh, but stops almost right away. "I could tell you stories! But I will spare you. Tell you what…"

"What?"

"I'll show you something." Ice gets up and closes the door. "But this is for your eyes only, man." He pulls his binder out of his drawer and holds it up. "Because there are no secrets between us roomies. Come on over." Ice waves at the line that still runs down the middle of the carpet. It's already faded in places. He runs his hands across the binder in his lap as gently as he stroked the horse's neck the other day. "Sit down, dude." Ice pats the covers next to him. "You ready?"

"Ready," says Knuckles McGraw, even though he doesn't know what he is ready for. He sits next to his bunkhouse buddy, feeling the warmth of Ice's arm against his.

CHAPTER 16

Iceberg Alley

Ice opens the binder slowly. The pages spread across both their laps.

Inside, the first page is covered with words all in the same spiky writing used on the sign over his bed. Knuckles McGraw reads them once. Then he reads them again more slowly to be sure he's got them right.

Icebergs:
Being the Definitive Study of Icebergs, their Origins,
Composition, Location and Physical Tendencies.
By Ian Cameron Emerson.
PRIVATE AND CONFIDENTIAL.

"Wow," says Knuckles McGraw.

"Wow is right, man," says Ice. "But you ain't seen nothing yet. There's facts here. They would take you a decade to find. I've used every source. There are statistics. Lists of names of icebergs…letters and numbers for each one, actually. Terminology. Eyewitness accounts." He flips a few more pages. "Scientific explanations. Pictures, of course. My best ones." He turns page after page. He slows down to look closely at some, turns the corner of one page as if to remember to go back to it.

Knuckles McGraw touches the edges with one finger. Then he turns to the front page again. "Is this your real name?" he asks.

"What?"

"This is your real name, isn't it?" He points at the words. "Ian Cameron Emerson. That spells Ice! I just figured it out."

"Well, you can just un-figure it." Ice slams the binder shut almost before Knuckles McGraw has a chance to take his hand away. He shoves it roughly into the drawer. "Get back on your side of the room. Go on! I show you something private, and you push your luck. No one calls me Ian. No one." He gives Knuckles McGraw a shove. "You wanna know the difference between private and secret? Private is stuff you shouldn't tell anyone about. Secrets are the stuff people stick their noses into anyway. Whether you want them to or not." Ice shoves him again.

Knuckles McGraw scurries across the room without checking that his feet don't touch the chalk line. He sits on his bed.

"Don't you dare tell anyone what you just saw," yells Ice. "Not anyone. Hear?" He comes right up close, so close his legs push against Knuckles McGraw's knees. When he looks down, his eyes are thin slits. "I thought you might be interested in my study. Icebergs are perhaps the most fascinating thing on this Earth. *Is that your real name*?" he imitates Knuckles McGraw's voice. "As if that has anything to do with anything. Keep your own secrets to yourself. And stay out of my private business."

He points to the chalk line. "You've probably never heard of Iceberg Alley. Well, this here is it. You know what happened to the *Titanic*? That's nothing compared to what will happen if you step just one foot over on my side."

Ice charges out of the room. The door slams behind him.

Knuckles McGraw's heart pounds like a drum in his chest as he listens to Ice charge down the stairs and out of the house, slamming the front door.

If Knuckles McGraw really was a cowboy, maybe he and Ice would have a shootout. Or maybe they'd wrestle in the dust until the sheriff pulled them apart. Even if he got dumped in jail for a day or two to cool off, he would ride out of town on Burlington Northern after he had done his time, and never look back.

He should have run away at the park, like he wanted to. But he didn't have the chance. The door was locked, and Ms. Havers was the only one who could let him out.

But his door is not locked now. It was easy enough for Ice to escape.

Maybe it's time for Knuckles McGraw to get out of town too.

CHAPTER 17

Runaway

He can hear the sound of the TV downstairs. Joe's and Liddy's voices mingle in the kitchen, all mixed up with the water running and dishes clattering.

If Burlington Northern were tied up outside, Knuckles McGraw could leap through the window right onto his back and gallop away before anyone knew he was gone. But for now, he has to creep down the stairs, avoiding the creaky ones, carrying his shoes in one hand and his lunch kit in the other. He shoves his shoes under his arm so he can turn the front-door handle. It opens without making a sound. He slinks down the porch stairs. The front path is damp. Cold seeps through his socks. But he won't stop to put on his shoes, not yet.

A man with an orange turban and a big black beard hurries past, loaded down with plastic shopping bags. A mom pushes a screaming baby in a stroller.

When he's safe around the corner, out of sight of the house, Knuckles McGraw sits on a bench at a bus stop to put on his shoes. Then he begins to run in the direction Joe takes them to school in the morning. Once he's there, he will be able to find the way to his own house.

As he heads across the crosswalk, he thinks he recognizes the band teacher in a car, waiting for the light to change. But he's not in band, so maybe she won't recognize him. He puts his head down and trots to the other side without looking back.

A banner is strung along the school fence. It says *Hall Road Elementary. Where Everyone Smiles in the Same Language.* Usually, when Knuckles McGraw sees it on his way into school, it makes him smile whether he feels like it or not.

It's almost dark when he gets to his own apartment building. Prem's windows are all dark. So he's probably either out at the temple or downstairs in the furnace room, where he has his workbench. From one window, Knuckles McGraw sees the blue glow from a TV.

Someone has their stereo up so loud that he can feel the thumping through his feet.

He heads up the stairs to his apartment and is about to dig for his key in the flowerpot when he hears voices from inside. He pushes on the door.

When it opens, he hears voices again. Not his mom's.

Maybe burglars! He stands very still listening hard. Then he hears a man's voice. He creeps along the hall, wishing he hadn't put his shoes back on.

"Sad state of affairs," says a lady's voice. It's Gloria. His grandmother!

"A home is a home. This is the boy's home," says his grandfather.

"...I always worried she'd do something..."

"We did what we could, Glo."

"He'll be fine once we get him..."

"...lots to keep him busy..."

Their words are all mixed-up with the sound of his grandpa's heavy feet, his grandma's high heels. Things being moved around. A cupboard opening.

He is listening hard and wondering why they are here when his grandpa comes out, taking up all the space in the doorway. "Look who's here. Gloria!"

"I thought you were burglars," says Knuckles McGraw.

"That nice man, Prim. Is that his name? He let us in." His grandma squeezes past his grandfather into the hall.

"I don't need anyone to let me in," he tells them. "I have my own key. This is my house. Why are you here?"

"We're just packing up a few things you might need when you come to stay with us," says his grandma.

"But I don't want to live with you. I want to stay here until my mom comes back."

Knuckles McGraw feels himself being led along by his grandpa's heavy hand on his shoulder. "Let's all calm down," his grandpa says.

The living room is tidier than it has ever been. The dresser top is bare; so is the coffee table. The afghan is folded neatly over the arm of a chair. A big blue suitcase he's never seen before lies open on the couch.

He closes the lid and keeps his hand on it. "I'm staying here until my mom comes to get me. It won't be long. I have stayed by myself before. Once for two nights…" He has just given away a secret he has never told anyone before. Not Joe and Liddy.

Not Ice when they were sharing private things in their bunkhouse. Especially not Ms. Havers, who tries to find out this kind of stuff about him and his mom.

He dashes into his bedroom. It's even tidier than he left it the day he went to school and found the note his mom had wrapped around his sandwich. He looks from one side of the room to the other.

It's not a bunkhouse, and there are no horses tied up outside. But here he does not have to share a room with a mean boy who will never melt.

Here, this room is all his own, and there's no one to make a big line down the middle to keep him on his own side.

Here is where his mom will expect to find him when she comes back. Even if he has to wait for days.

CHAPTER 18

A Real Rodeo Rider

"Kevin?" His grandfather pokes his head around the door. "Can I come in?" The bed squeals when he sits. "We really thought you might stay with us for a while. Give us the chance to get to know each other."

"I have to stay here for when my mom comes back." He's under his top covers with his shoes still on.

"You know you can't be left here alone."

"I need to be here so my mom knows where to find me."

"Kevin, you can't stay by yourself," says his grandpa again. "And if you're at your new friends' house, how will she know you are there?"

He sits up. What will happen if his mom comes here and doesn't find him and doesn't know he's just across town? "That's why I have to stay right here!"

His grandfather walks around his room slowly. He looks at the *Star Wars* poster on the wall and then pushes around the leftover Lego pieces on the dresser. "Do you mind if I call you Kevin?" asks his grandfather. "That's how we have thought of you all these years. Even though Knuckles McGraw is a wonderful name for a cowboy."

Words he thought were private, that Knuckles McGraw had kept a secret, suddenly fly out of his mouth. "I could be a cowboy," he says. "I have a horse, you know."

"You do?"

"Yes. Well. Kind of."

"Kind of how?" When his grandpa frowns, the wrinkles go all the way up to the top of his head, like little ripples in water when you throw a rock in.

"He's not quite real. But he's my constant companion. When times are tough and the tough get going, we head out onto the range." Knuckles McGraw has told his story to himself so many times, but it hardly sounds right when he says it aloud. "We sleep under the stars. And I make coffee over the campfire. I don't really like coffee, but when I'm a cowboy I drink it. And no one can catch us even though we're on the run. It's just me and my horse. Under the big sky." He's run out of breath, and he sits up straighter to get more air into him. "Just Knuckles McGraw and Burlington Northern."

His grandpa's voice is quiet. "Is that what you call him?"

"Everyone else has to call him that. I call him Burlington for short."

"That's some name." The chair next to his bed creaks as his grandfather sinks onto it slowly. "Knuckles McGraw and Burlington Northern." He rubs his knees with his big hands. "I've heard some wild cowboy stories in my time. That sounds like one of the best. 'The Ballad of Knuckles McGraw.' That's what we'd call your story if it was a song."

"'The Ballad of Knuckles McGraw.'" He echoes his grandfather's words. "But Burlington Northern would have to be in it too."

"That goes without saying. Sounds like what you need is to get a horse under you. See what it's really like with your feet in the stirrups."

"I've never been on a horse."

"Sure you have. In a manner of speaking."

"I don't think so," says Knuckles McGraw.

"Don't you remember?" his grandpa asks.

"My dad once rode me around the room on his back. He wore a hat, so you could hardly see his face."

"That wasn't your dad, son."

"Not my dad?"

"That was me. Your old grandpa, here."

"That's not true!"

"Roper Mason. That's my rodeo name."

"No way."

"Yes way!" says his grandpa. "It's true. Sure as I'm sitting here, next to my grandson at last." He sits back and grins at Knuckles McGraw, as if he is expecting him to argue.

But all he can say is, "Wow." If his grandfather is a rodeo rider, he must know how to jump on a horse when it is still moving and head onto the range without looking back. Maybe he has slept under the big sky with only a campfire glowing in the dark. "That's a cool cowboy name." Knuckles McGraw climbs out of bed and stands in front of his grandpa, Roper Mason.

"Glad you like it."

"I thought my dad was a cowboy," he tells him. "I thought I remembered him riding me around on his back. He sang cowboy songs." He watches his grandpa, who is smiling so hard. "Was that you too?" Knuckles McGraw asks.

"That was me, sure enough. Down on my knees, I was. And you just a little tot. You hung onto my shirt for dear life." He rubs his hand over his head. Front to back, then back again. "Even grabbed my hair, in the days I still had some."

"And you sang me songs too?"

"I did. I did. 'The Streets of Laredo.' 'Tumbling Tumbleweeds.' Sometimes even ones I made up myself."

"One with *Yippie Ya Yay*?"

"'My Little Cowgirl,' that would be." Roper Mason puts his head back and roars, "*Yippie-ki-yo-yippie-yay, L'il Momma, Yippie-ki-yo-yippie-yay, L'il Momma, Yippie-ki-yo-yippie-yay.*"

"Sing it again."

His grandpa pats his chest. "I'm about all out of breath. I'm not much for singing anymore. And these fingers are too stiff to do much with a guitar these days.

But I still write a cowboy song from time to time to remind me of the old days."

Just then Grandma Gloria comes into the room. "You two are making enough racket," she says. "You need to make sure there's nothing else you want to take with you." She looks at Knuckles McGraw carefully. "That is, if you've decided to come home with your grandpa and me."

Grandma Gloria and Grandpa Lyle are both watching him, waiting for him to make up his mind.

It's up to him.

It's up to him if he stays or goes. And to decide if he goes back to being Kevin Mason, or sticks with Knuckles McGraw, ready to leave town at a moment's notice.

"It would just be until your mom comes back, mind," says his grandpa. "She will come looking for you when she's ready. And when she does, we'll make sure she finds out where you are."

"Safe and sound with us, Kevin," says his grandma, like she's used to finishing his grandpa's thoughts.

Maybe Edmonton is not such a bad place to be while he waits for his mom to remember to come back to get him.

Even with a long duster that hangs over his boots and a battered hat on his head, it's still cold out there on the range for a cowboy all alone with only his horse. When his grandma called him Kevin, for the first time in days it sounded just fine. Knuckles McGraw thinks he remembers what it felt like to be Kevin Mason, laughing as he rode around the room on his grandfather's back, slithering and sliding. First one way, then another. Holding on for dear life.

And he thinks he remembers something else. When he did fall off, his grandfather was there to pick him right up and put him back and start all over again.

CHAPTER 19

A Ballad for Kevin Mason

For the next few days, while his grandpa and grandma—who say he can call them Gloria and Lyle if he likes—are busy with the welfare lady, and at his old apartment, Kevin hangs out with Liddy. When he helps her refinish a table, she lets him hold the sander with her hand on his to guide it around and around. That night at supper, little specks of sawdust fall from his hair into his soup.

One day Ice takes him over to the equestrian center. He sits on a bale of hay and plays with the kittens while Ice cleans out the stalls and leads the horses out to the fields one by one, walking slowly by Kevin each time so he can get used to them.

He doesn't ask to see Ice's binder again. It's private, even if it's not a secret anymore. And even though he knows Ice's real name now, he's not about to tell anyone else! Roommates always have secrets.

In the mornings and after school, Breezy still spends a lot of time doing handstands against the wall. One day he sees she has painted all her toes the same orange color as the lipstick his grandma wears all day, every day. But although he listens hard, Kevin never hears Breezy speak again.

"She will when she's ready," Liddy tells him. He's sorry he won't be there to hear it.

The day Ms. Havers talked to him in her car, she said that one day Ice would melt and not be so tough. Kevin hopes Breezy will melt enough to talk one day, when she gets over being sad that her parents died. Like he got used to the fact his mother left him just for now, and he doesn't need to be Knuckles McGraw anymore.

His grandma and grandpa have decided to drive him and all his stuff back to Alberta. There's just room for Kevin to squeeze into the back seat of the car with his lunch box at his feet. His mom's letter is still in there, along with two books, a pack of cards and some snacks for when he gets hungry. And the picture of him and his mom at the Bear Creek Park train.

When they're ready to leave, Kevin and the grown-ups stand around saying awkward goodbyes. Breezy does cartwheels along the sidewalk, giving her little finger wave when she finally stops, all out of breath.

"Hey, Knuckles McGraw!"

Kevin looks up to see Ice hanging out of the bedroom window.

"Yeah, you. I'm talking to you, Knuckles McGraw," Ice yells again. When he throws something out of the window, it comes sailing down in a wide swoop.

"I told you. I'm Kevin Mason now," he yells back as he picks up the paper at his feet. It's an airplane, made from the iceberg picture that Ice put on his wall the day he drew the chalk line down the middle of the room. The picture he stole from the library copy of *National Geographic*.

Kevin Mason will never tell. He folds it back up into its plane shape. One more thing to save in his lunch box. He waves. "Thanks, Ice."

But Knuckles McGraw's bunkhouse buddy has already pulled his head back in, and the window is closed again.

When all the hugging and kissing is over, Grandpa Lyle checks his watch. "There's a quick detour we need to make on our way out of town. Isn't there, Kevin?"

"Sure is."

"No rush at all, dear," says Grandma. "We have all the time in the world."

Grandpa stops by the side of the road at the railroad crossing to wait for the white arm to come down, its light flashing and little bell ringing.

Kevin twists in his seat one way. No train in sight. When he turns the other way, he can just see the big engine coming closer between the shrubs along the track. They sit in silence, just the way he did not long ago with the welfare lady beside him. When he had no idea how things would turn out.

"Here she comes," says Grandpa as the train starts to rattle by. "If we're going to count the boxcars, we better start now."

But Kevin is too busy studying their rusty red sides to keep count. One after the other they pass by, with all kinds of writing on them. At last, he sees what he's been waiting for. "Look!"

"Darn. Now I'll never get caught up," says Grandpa Lyle. "I only got to twenty-three. And they're still coming."

"Look!"

His grandma sets her needlepoint in her lap. His grandpa leans forward over the steering wheel and squints through the front window.

There, written in white letters on the ribby sides of boxcar after boxcar are the words, *Burlington Northern. Burlington Northern. Burlington Northern. Burlington Northern. Burlington Northern.*

"I'll be darned," says his grandpa with a husky laugh. "Don't they look just like a herd of horses being led back to the corral? Rocking along behind each other. Burlington Northern. Burlington for short! A perfect name for a horse."

"I can't see my name," says Kevin. His eyes search back and forth, looking for Knuckles McGraw, written in graffiti. But he didn't really expect to find it. He no longer knows if he really saw it there. Or if he made it up.

The caboose is coming along now. So Kevin Mason waves at the trainman, who sits with his arm hanging out of the grimy window. Just like he always does.

And this time the man waves back! Waving goodbye to Knuckles McGraw, maybe. Kevin's grandpa waits for the train to rumble away, getting smaller and smaller, heading out of town as fast as it can go, before he starts the car.

As they all watch the train disappear into the distance, his grandfather asks, "Anyone for a song?"

"What song should we start with, dear?" Grandma Gloria smiles at Kevin through the rearview mirror, like she's been keeping a secret and he's about to find out what it is.

" 'The Ballad of Knuckles McGraw,' " announces Grandpa. "Written specially for my favorite grandson. There's no music yet. That can come later." He turns and winks at Kevin. "We have all the time in the world."

As they drive away, heading to Edmonton, Alberta, where his mom will find him when she's ready to come looking, Kevin sits back in his seat.

He listens to every word as his grandfather recites the ballad he made up just for him.

"The Ballad of Knuckles McGraw"

Words and music by Douglas H. Brunt

Sit for a spell and I'll tell you a tale
Of a cowboy named Knuckles McGraw,
A two-fisted rider as brave as they come,
The toughest man you ever saw.

Knuckles McGraw was a man with few friends
Till one day he met up with a horse.
A friendship was born out of mutual need
And together they plotted their course.

Burlington Northern's the name of his mount,
A stallion who's sixteen hands high.
In the dark of the night, put your ear to the ground,
You can hear the pair thundering by.

They travel like wind when the moon lights their way
Across the wild plains t'ward the sun.
They ride for adventure to hell and beyond,
They ride till their journey is done.

Knuckles McGraw is a man without ties;
He searched through the long lonely night.
When he found all the answers he needed to know,
He fixed all the wrongs; now they're right.

Burlington Northern and Knuckles McGraw
Finally came to the end of their road.
Together they'd fixed up all that they could;
It was time that they put down their load.

When Knuckles McGraw said goodbye to his horse
With a whistle, a wink, and a wave,
Burlington Northern took off in a flash
To new friends and others to save.

But Burlington Northern still runs like the wind,
The stallion who's sixteen hands high.
In the dark of the night, put your ear to the ground,
You can still hear him thundering by.

The Ballad of Knuckles McGraw

Words and Music by Douglas H. Brunt

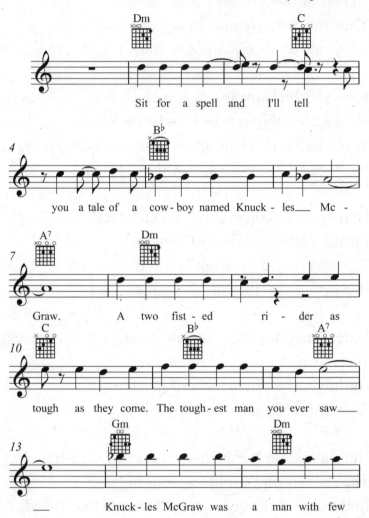

friends till   one   day he met up   with a   horse____

A friend - ship was   born out   of   mu - tual need.

To -   gether they plotted their course.

Acknowledgments

Many thanks to the keen eye, light touch and kind heart of my editor (and an awesome writer herself) Sarah Harvey at Orca. And a special nod to all the publishers, editors, teachers, librarians and teacher-librarians everywhere who work so hard to put the right book in the right child's hands at the right time.

And this time, special thanks to Knuckles McGraw's official First Kid Reader, Isaiah!

As always, my husband Douglas Brunt encouraged my writing, and wrote the ballad.

Lois Peterson's first Orca Young Reader was *Meeting Miss 405*. The idea for *The Ballad of Knuckles McGraw* came to her as she sat watching a Burlington Northern train judder across the railway crossing in Surrey, where she lives and works.

Lois wrote for adults for many years before turning to writing kids' books in 2007. She is also a writing instructor and, in 2009, founded the Surrey Writers' School.

Ten percent of author royalties from all of her books go to charity; revenues from this book will help the programs for young children provided through Alexandra Neighbourhood House in Surrey.

Visit her website at www.loispeterson.net.

Also by Lois Peterson:

Meeting Miss 405

978-1-55469-015-2
$7.95 pb · 112 pages

Life is hard for Tansy with her depressed mom away indefinitely and her dad making a mess of things at home. Things don't seem to get any better when she gets sent to Miss Stella, a wrinkly old babysitter from down the hall. Miss Stella has a unique perspective on life, to say the least, but Tansy gradually learns to manage all the changes in her life and make unexpected new friends in the process.